101 AMAZING

MYTHICAL BEASTS

...and Legendary Creatures

Jack Goldstein

Published in 2014 by
AUK Authors, an imprint of
Andrews UK Limited
www.andrewsuk.com

Contents

Introduction

Did you know that a Hippogriff is supposedly the offspring of a horse and a griffin? Or that a Greek Sphinx generally has a male face, whereas an Egyptian one has a female visage? Where does the Skunk Ape roam, and how can you spot a Kitsune in human form? Is Slenderman the most frightening mythical creature, or is that honour bestowed on the fearsome Gashadokuro? This fantastic book contains details of over one hundred mythical beasts and legendary creatures, organised into categories for easy reference. Whether you are interested in the beasts of anywhere from Ancient Greece to modern-day Africa, this is the book for you!

101 Amazing Mythical Beasts

Classical - Part 1

1. **Salamander:** Although this species of *Urodela* (amphibians with a lizard-like appearance) is certainly real, the classical civilizations believed they had occult properties. For instance, although Pliny the elder was smart enough to distinguish the Salamander from actual lizards (in a taxonomical sense), he also held a belief that they could extinguish fire with their bodies. The *Talmud* (a Jewish Rabbinic text) states that smearing yourself in the blood of a salamander will make you immune from fire, and some believed that the creature was so poisonous that just by climbing around a tree it would poison its fruit so badly that anyone who ate even a single bite would perish immediately.

2. **Phoenix:** The ancients believed that when it was a Phoenix's time to die, it would be consumed by flames and burn to a pile of ashes. From these embers the bird would be reborn, continuing an eternal cycle of death and rebirth. Believed to have been colourful and vibrant (although some believed it was red, others purple and a few even blue), the bird was said to be anything between the size of an eagle and an ostrich! Interestingly, there appear to be Phoenix parallels in many cultures, from the *Firebird* of Russia to the Turkish *Kerkes*, the *Fenghuang* of China, the Hindu *Anka* and more.

3.   **Faun:** Half human and half goat, the Faun of classical mythology is often related to the wood-god Pan. Sometimes considered friendly (helping lost humans in need) but other times evil (causing intense fear in travellers in remote woodland locations), the creatures are often depicted in art playing the flute.

4.   **Centaur:** Perhaps one of the best-known of all creatures of classical mythology, the Centaur has the head, arms and torso of a man attached to the body and legs of a horse. Depicted most often as noble creatures (yet occasionally as the very embodiment of untamed nature) they are almost always male; female Centaurs are generally known as kentaurides.

5.   **Werewolf:** Although belief in a human/wolf hybrid was popularised in Europe in the middle ages, there are plenty of references to this beast in classical literature. For instance, a tribe called the *Neuri* were said to all have the ability to transform into wolves for several days each year, and Pliny tells us of how one man transformed into a wolf after placing his clothes on an ash tree and swimming across a lake. Admittedly however, it was around 1500 years later that the legend of the Werewolf took the form we know today, with subjects inflicted with the condition after being bitten. In some legends, the ability to transform is optional, whereas in others it is forced upon the subject when the moon is full. However most sources agree that a Werewolf can be killed by a silver bullet (or silver-tipped arrow).

6. **Harpy:** Appearing in both Greek and Roman mythology, the Harpies were birds with female human faces. Although in the earliest writings we have found, the creatures' appearance is described as 'beautiful', public opinion seems to have changed over the years - and by Roman times they were said to be hideously ugly. According to Virgil, there were three Harpies - *Aello* (meaning 'storm swift'), *Ocypete* ('the swift wing') and *Calaeno* ('the dark'). The awful creatures remained present in leading literature for over a thousand years, with Dante's *Inferno* (written in the middle ages) detailing how those who have committed suicide face their punishment in a tortured wood infested with Harpies.

7. **Cerberus:** Also known as the *Hellhound*, this multi-headed dog with a mane of snakes, the tail of a serpent and the claws of a lion guarded the entrance to the underworld and was responsible for preventing the living from entering - and the dead from escaping! There is much debate about the number of heads that Cerberus possessed; whereas the general consensus is three, some sources say two, and still others suggest as many as one hundred! Whereas Orpheus is said to have coaxed Cerberus into slumber with music, Virgil's *Aeneid* tells of how he was lulled into a deep sleep after eating drugged honeycakes.

8. **Minotaur:** Half bull and half man, this creature was said to dwell in the middle of the *Labyrinth*; a maze on the island of Crete. Interestingly, there seems

to be some disagreement between authors as to which half of the creature was which; whilst today we generally picture it as having the head of a bull but the body of a man, there is plenty of literature from the middle ages which depicts the reverse, more akin to a Centaur! In classical mythology, the Minotaur was eventually slain by Theseus.

9.   **Unicorn:** The belief in Unicorns - essentially white or silver horses with a single horn on their head - dates back thousands of years, even before Greek and Roman times. The bible itself mentions a creature of this description called the *re'em*, which in many translations is called a Unicorn. Interestingly, the Greeks did not consider the Unicorn a mythological animal - they were absolutely convinced it existed in India. The animal was even described in intricate detail, including its call (which was said to be a deep lowing noise). In the middle ages, people believed the Unicorn to be more of a woodland animal, one that could only be captured by a virgin! In reading ancient descriptions of the Unicorn in more detail, some today have suggested that they might actually refer to the rhinoceros; strange as though this may sound, read what you may from this quote from Marco Polo that Unicorns are: "scarcely smaller than elephants. They have the hair of a buffalo and feet like an elephant's. They have a single large black horn in the middle of the forehead... They have a head like a wild boar's... They spend their time by preference wallowing in mud and slime. They are very ugly brutes to look at."

10. **Griffin:** Often also spelt *Gryphon*, this creature has the body, tail and back legs of a lion, but the head, wings and front legs of an eagle. The Griffin was believed to be powerful and majestic, combining the nature of the kings of the beasts and of the birds. They were always said to guard treasure or possessions of untold wealth. Interestingly, belief in the creature dates back over five thousand years, with some historians speculating that ancient Egyptian and Persian people may have misidentified dinosaur remains found near a gold mine!

Cerberus

European - Part 1

11. **Ceffyl Dŵr:** This Welsh water horse has the power not only to shape-shift at will, but also to fly. Some people say one can feel when Ceffyl Dŵr is nearby due to its foreboding presence and that you must never look into its fiery eyes, whereas others say he is purely a cheeky pest who playfully swims in mountain pools and over waterfalls. It is said that if you approach Ceffyl Dŵr, one of two things will happen - either it will evaporate into the mist, or it will jump out of the water and trample you to death.

12. **Hippogriff:** First described fully in the 16th century, the Hippogriff is said to be the offspring of a horse and a *Griffin*; it is essentially a winged horse with the head and shoulders of an eagle. Apparently able to fly to the moon and back, the Hippogriff is extremely fast and can only be ridden by magicians.

13. **Wyvern:** This beast has a reptile's body, two feet and a Dragon's head and tail. If you pay attention to European coats of arms, you will come across this creature quite often; it is even thought to have been the symbol of the medieval kingdom of Wessex. Another common place for the Wyvern to appear is on the badge of athletics teams in both Europe and America. According to legend, you may - if you are lucky enough - come across a *Sea-Wyvern*, which sports a fish's tail rather than that of a Dragon and is (of course) water-dwelling.

14. **Barbegazi:** Featuring in French and Swiss mythology, the Barbegazi are small white-furred gnomes that sport extremely long beards and enormous feet which they use as skis to navigate around their mountain homeland. These creatures hibernate during the warmer summer months and are rarely sighted by humans - except to help round up lost sheep or warn of an impending avalanche by whistling.

15. **Ant Lion:** Sometimes referred to as *Myrmecoleon* or *Formicaleon*, there are supposedly two forms of Ant Lion. One is the result of a lion mating with an ant, having the face of the former and the body of the latter. In this configuration, because the lion part can only eat meat yet the ant part can only digest grain, the creature starves to death after being born. On the other hand, some say it is a huge ant that hides amongst dust before jumping out to hunt other ants. This is perhaps one of the strangest hybrid creatures in the medieval bestiaries!

16. **Shug Monkey:** Living between Balsham and West Wrattling in Cambridgeshire, this cryptid has an ape-like body and head, but huge paws more akin to a dog. Locals say they have seen the beast walking on all fours, but when approached it faded away like a dissolving apparition. Little is known of the origin of the Shug Monkey - even the etymology is unknown - although some believe the myth dates back to Norse settlers from over a thousand years ago.

17. **Owlman:** It is 1976 and a man by the name of Don Melling is taking a holiday in Cornwall with his two daughters. Walking past Mawnan church, the girls look up and see a terrifying sight - a cross between a man and an owl hovering around the belltower. Running to their father they abandon their holiday and drive back to Lancaster. If you find this hard to believe, perhaps the second sighting that came two months later will convince you... a fourteen year old girl reported seeing a huge owl as big as a man with pointed ears and red eyes whilst camping in woods close to the church. Still not enough? Over the next two years, more and more people reported seeing what came to be dubbed *Owlman*, with no explanation offered other than the supernatural or paranormal. Interestingly, in 1989, over a decade after talk of the monster had subsided, a witness described having seen a very similar beast in the area; one which five years later a visitor from Chicago also saw...

18. **Grim:** Also known as *Padfoot, Shag* and *Skriker*, there are tales across most of Europe that refer to this blackest of dogs. Some say that seeing one is a sure sign of impending doom, whereas others tell tales of a ghost who barks throughout the night but causes harm to none. Perhaps the strangest *Black Dog* legend is in Devon, where the headless *Yeth Hound* (said to be the spirit of an unbaptised child) prowls through woodland, all the time a-wailing.

19. **Salmon of Knowledge:** Also known as *Fintan mac Bóchra*, this 'big fish' of Irish legend gained all the world's knowledge by eating nine hazelnuts from nine different trees that surrounded the *Well of Wisdom*. Anyone who found the fish and subsequently cooked and ate it would themselves gain all of this knowledge - and according to the stories, a servant boy called Fionn did just that.

20. **Reynardine:** Mentioned commonly in English ballads of Victorian times, this *Werefox* is said to attract beautiful women to him who he then captures, taking them to his castle of bones. Worryingly, no original source ever tells us what happens to the women once they reach their destination - perhaps every single one of them is still there, wherever it is!

A Hippogriff

African

21. **Anansi:** This West African God most often takes the form of a spider, although sometimes appears as a man. Some people even tell tales of him appearing as a spider with clothes, or as a man with eight legs! He is the stereotypical trickster, always gaining the upper hand with his guile and cunning. Although mischievous, Anansi is in fact good, acting on behalf of his father *Nyame*, the Sky God. It is said that Anansi brought all of the stories into the world.

22. **Emela Ntouka:** In Central Africa, Pygmy tribes speak of the *Emela-Ntouka*, an elephant-sized creature with a body and head (including horn) of a rhinoceros, yet possessing a much heavier tail. Inhabiting the swamps and lakes of the Congo, Cameroon and Zambia, the creature is greatly feared - even though it is said to be herbivorous.

23. **Ngoloko:** Also known as the *Nandi Bear*, this beast - similar in nature (although not necessarily in appearance) to a *Yeti* - is said to live in western Kenya. With high front shoulders and a sloping back similar to that of a hyena, descriptions of this beast most closely resemble an extinct species called *Chalicotherium*. As with many cryptids, one wonders whether a species has truly become extinct, or if there is a possibility that a small pack or community has continued living in secret to this day.

24. **Inkanyamba:** The Zulu tribes of Pietermaritzburg in South Africa tell tales of a huge serpent with a horse's head that lives in a waterfall lake underneath the Howick Falls. The beast's anger is said to be responsible for storm activity during the summer months.

25. **Mbielu-Mbielu-Mbielu:** If you are knowledgeable about dinosaurs, have a go at naming one that fits the description of the *Mbielu-Mbielu-Mbielu*... 'a four-legged herbivorous beast roughly ten metres long with a short neck, a medium sized tail and planks covered in green algae growing out of its back'. If you instantly thought 'stegosaurus' then you are in agreement with many who have studied the tale of this creature. It originates from the Republic of the Congo and has been seen only near two villages - Bounila and Ebolo.

26. **Ninki Nanka:** This Dragon-like creature of West African folklore is large and dangerous. Inhabiting the swamps of the region, the beast eats children who disobey their parents by venturing into its territory. A number of people claim to have seen the *Ninki Nanka,* and as recently as 2006 there have been expeditions to Gambia to try and find the monster.

27. **Jengu:** The Sawa people of Cameroon have legends that tell of mermaid-like figures who live in both fresh and saltwater. With gap-toothed smiles and long woolly hair they bring good fortune (such as curing disease) to those who worship them.

28. **Popobawa:** Should you be sitting outside your homestead on the Tanzanian island of Pemba late one night, and begin to smell a strange sulphurous odour, it is time to run or fight - Popobawas are about to attack. These terrifying shape-shifters most often take the form of giant bats, although they can transmute at will between this and human form. Belief in the Popobawas continues to this day in the region, and as recently as 2007 there were mass panics due to reported attacks by these awful beasts. Should you be the subject of their wrath, you are forced to tell your friends - as the Popobawas will continue their visits to you if you not do so.

29. **Mokele-mbembe:** Whereas *Mbielu-Mbielu-Mbielu* is said to resemble a stegosaurus, *Mokele-mbembe* has the appearance of a sauropod such as a diplodocus. Dwelling in the waters of the Congo River basin, there have been many real-life expeditions to try and spot the creature, none successful. Similar in nature to the stories of the *Loch Ness Monster*, one must wonder whether it is truly possible for a species of dinosaur to have survived into the modern day in one of the least explored areas on the planet...

30. **Rompo:** Perhaps one of the most interesting 'hybrid' animal legends of Africa, the Rompo has the head of a hare (but with the ears of a human), a skeletal body, the front arms of a badger and the hind legs of a bear. The only food this creature eats is human corpses, and when it does find a tasty morsel it sings as it swallows the sweet dead flesh.

Mokele-mbembe

Asian

31. **Jorōgumo:** Beware if you are taking a walk in rural regions of Japan and you see a beautiful woman playing a lute - she could be a *Jorōgumo*. Once you have been enticed into a shack by her beauty and by the soothing song, she will turn into a spider, bind you in silk and devour you entirely. In some stories, the woman even carries a bundle that initially appears to be a baby, but on closer inspection is actually a spider egg from which hundreds of spider children will burst before feeding on your succulent flesh.

32. **Kitsune:** Commonly spoken of in Japanese folklore, Kitsune are essentially foxes that can take human form. Divided into two types - *zenko* (benevolent spirits) and *yako* (those that are mischievous and malicious), all Kitsune are said to be highly intelligent and possess magical powers. The older and more powerful a Kitsune becomes, the more tails it grows - up to a maximum of nine, at which point its fur becomes white or gold and it gains the ability to see or hear anything that is happening anywhere in the entire world. Before transforming into a human, the Kitsune must place a reed or broad leaf on its head, and even after transformation the spirit may not be able to shed its tail - spotting this should a Kitsune get drunk or careless is a common way to discern its true nature.

33. **Longma:** In Chinese mythology, the Longma was a winged horse covered with Dragon scales. The word itself means Dragon (long) horse (ma). If a Longma was seen, most people believed it was an omen that a great and wise ruler would soon come to power.

34. **Ahool:** In the deepest rainforests of Java lives a giant bat with a wingspan of over three metres. Covered in grey fur and with large claws on its forearms, some even believe this creature - the Ahool - to resemble a pterosaur.

35. **Uchchaihshravas:** Snow white in colour, Uchchaihshravas us a seven-headed horse in Hindu mythology that possesses the ability of flight. Although some tales tell of this king of horses being a vehicle of *Indra* (the god-king of heaven), others state that it is in fact the horse of *Bali*, king of demons.

36. **Rokurokubi:** Initially, these Japanese phantoms look no different to humans - until either their necks stretch to ridiculous lengths, or their heads in fact detach entirely from their bodies and float around! Usually female in form, these spirits are often said to be malevolent, attacking humans at night. Some studies from the Edo period (roughly the 17th and 18th centuries in Japan) suggested that some Rokurokubi were not in fact *Yōkai* (a word meaning phantom or spirit) but were humans who suffered from a physical condition that caused their necks to stretch whilst they slept.

37. **Baku:** Possessing an elephant's trunk, an ox's tail, a tiger's paws and the eyes of a rhinoceros, the Baku devours dreams and thus prevents one from having nightmares. In more recent years, naturalists have noted the similarity between the description of the Baku and real-world animal the tapir.

38. **Jiangshi:** A truly terrifying creature, the Jiangshi is a stiff human corpse dressed in the official garments of the Qing dynasty. Always with its arms outstretched, this zombie moves by hopping, seeking out living creatures at night and devouring their life-force. During the day, the Jiangshi rests in either a coffin or in a dark, dank cave. Some Jiangshi look almost like you or I (as they are the corpse of the recently deceased), whereas others (who have been decomposing for some time) have rotting flesh hanging off their yellowing bones.

39. **Ox-Head** and **Horse-Face:** The first two people that dead souls meet when arriving in the Chinese underworld (where they are tortured prior to being reincarnated) are Ox-Head and Horse-Face. These guardians of the realm are exactly as their names would suggest - one has the head of an ox on the body of a man, whereas the other has the face of a horse. On very rare occasions, souls are said to have escaped from the underworld, but they are spotted by the far-seeing eyes of *Yama* and the two guardians are sent to retrieve (and punish) the escapees.

40.   **Yamata no Orochi:** With eights heads and eight tails, the Japanese Dragon Yamata no Orochi was slain by *Susanoo*, the storm god of Shinto legend; the beast had lived in the Hii river in Izumo Province, and every year had demanded (and received) the sacrifice of a daughter of two earthly deities.

A Kitsune

Modern Day

41. **Trunko:** In 1924 witnesses saw an unusual creature in the sea off the coast of Margate in South Africa. After a battle to the death with two killer whales, the carcass of this unusual animal washed up on the beach. Those who saw both the fight and the subsequent carcass say that it was even larger that the killer whales themselves (although succumbed due to being outnumbered), was covered in snowy-white fur, and possessed the trunk of an elephant and a lobster-like tail so powerful it had slapped one whale twenty feet into the air. Dubbed *Trunko*, the creature was thought to be a local urban legend until four photographs of the unusual carcass turned up years later!

42. **Gef:** In 1930s Britain, one animal from a species that scientists knew existed became the subject of widespread zoological press reports - a mongoose called Gef. What was particularly unusual however was that this mongoose could talk. Living in a farmhouse on the Isle of Man, the creature said that he was born in New Delhi in India in 1852 and was in fact an 'invisible ghost mongoose'. When asked what he looked like, Gef said that if you saw him you would be turned into a pillar or stone or salt. Proof of Gef's existence was never found, and some accused the family of perpetrating a hoax - fuelled by one investigator's belief that the daughter used ventriloquism to fool people into thinking they had heard Gef's voice from elsewhere!

43. **Bigfoot:** Also known as *Sasquatch*, this ape-like creature is reported to have been seen in the Pacific Northwest region of America. Although the indigenous population of the area have told of wild men in the folklore for hundreds of years, many scientists believe bigfoot to be purely a hoax perpertrated by locals. On the other hand, there has been some evidence in support of the cryptid actually being real. Most famously, in 1967 two men claimed to have captured a specimen on video; this footage can be widely viewed and is known as the *Patterson-Gimlin film*. This was proof plenty for believers, however detractors of the creature's existence claim it is purely a man in an ape-suit. The subject of a 2007 photograph taken by a motion-triggered camera attached to a tree was also dismissed as 'not Bigfoot' by the state's Game Commission who declared the animal seen is probably 'a bear with mange'.

44. **The Loch Ness Monster:** One of the world's most famous cryptids, this beast inhabits Loch Ness in the Scottish Highlands (*Loch* being the Scottish word for a lake or sea inlet). Over the years there has been much 'evidence' put forward of Nessie (as the creature has come to be known) including photographs, film and even sonar scans. Generally, the monster is considered to be a hump-backed water creature, with many speculating that it could be a plesiosaur (or more likely a family of this or similar species) that has survived since the dinosaur age.

45. **Yeti:** Also known as the *Abominable Snowman*, this creature is one legendary beast that a wide number of scientists believe may truly be real. Living in the Himalayas (around Nepal and Tibet) and resembling a large ape that walks on two feet like a human, the creature has been part of local mythology for hundreds of years, and became known across the wider world in the late 19th century. Samples of animal material such as fur have actually been found in the region and have been subjected to DNA tests and other scientific analysis. The results of these have surprised many - the DNA matched that of an ancient polar bear that lived one hundred thousand years ago. It is therefore highly possible that the Yeti of today could exist as a species not found elsewhere in the world, having evolved into the rarely seen beast.

46. **Melon Heads:** In Michigan, Ohio and Connecticut, in recent years people have spoken in hushed voices of the *Melon Heads* or *Wobble Heads*, humanoids with bulbous heads who - when they cannot secretly forage enough food for sustenance - emerge from their hiding places to attack locals. Some say the Melon Heads are people on whom terrible experiments were conducted who (after slaying their captor) now lead a feral existence, whereas others believe their terrifying appearance is due to generations of cannibalism. The legend of these creatures became so well known that a film about them was made!

47. **Mothman:** Between 1966 and 1967, a huge man-like creature - but with the wings of a moth - was seen by a number of witnesses in the Point Pleasant area of West Virginia. It was speculated (in John Keel's 1975 book *The Mothman Prophecies*) that the creature was part of a host of other supernatural events in the area at the time. The sightings were (of course) played down by the country sheriff, who suggested people might have seen 'a rather large heron' and become confused.

48. **The Hodag:** In 1893, local newspapers in Wisconsin published a photograph of what appeared to be a gruesome creature with the head of a frog (on which sat the face of an elephant), supported by thick legs at the end of which were huge claws. The beast had the back of a dinosaur and a tail which sported spears at its end. Although the man who began the expedition to capture this strange animal - called a Hodag - eventually 'admitted' its existence was a hoax, some have speculated he only did this to protect the remaining members of its species who live on to this very day...

49. **The Loveland Frog:** This modern-day legend hails from Ohio and has been spotted on a number of occasions. Witnesses say the creature is four feet tall and takes the form of a frog, but with the face of a human. Perhaps inhabiting the nearby Little Miami River, the Frog (also sometimes referred to as the *Loveland Lizard*) is surely a disturbing sight!

50. **The Beast of Bodmin Moor:** After farmers in Cornwall discovered their livestock mutilated, a number of theories were put forward. One that quickly rose in popularity was that an escaped wildcat may have been hunting for prey. Despite this explanation being rejected by scientists (due to their belief that larger species of cat could not survive outdoors throughout England's cold winters), the theory had gained a strong foothold and the legend was born. The beast is just one example of what are called *Phantom Cats* or *Alien Big Cats* - essentially species believed to be living in an area to which they are not native. The legend of the Beast of Bodmin Moor gained such notoriety that the United Kingdom Ministry of Agriculture conducted an official investigation in 1995, and although they could not prove the cat's existence, they stated explicitly that it *was* a possibility!

A Hodag

General

51. **Dragon:** Almost every culture across the world features Dragons in its mythology. This interesting 'convergence of myth' has led many to propose that Dragons were in fact at one time real - otherwise how would belief in them have been so widespread?! Generally seen as reptilian beasts with wings (and often the ability to breathe fire) there are plenty of 'real world' theories as to their origin, from huge lizards (such as the Komodo Dragon of today) to spitting cobras, Nile crocodiles and more.

52. **Bunyip:** In Aboriginal mythology, the Bunyip would lurk in waterholes, creeks and riverbeds. Descriptions of its appearance vary significantly across Australia, ranging from a hybrid with the face of a dog, head of a crocodile, tail of a horse and bill of a duck to an 'enormous starfish' according to the Moorundi people. In 1847, a skull purporting to have belonged to a Bunyip was displayed in the Australian Museum, although experts dismissed it as belonging to a deformed calf.

53. **Manananggal:** If you're in the Philippines, beware of the Manananggal. A hideous female form with bat-like wings, this blood-sucker mostly prays on pregnant women, using its tube-like tongue to suck out the heart of the unborn foetus.

54.   **Ponaturi:** Maori legend tells of the Ponaturi, a group of goblins who by day live in a land under the sea, and at night return to sleep by the shore. The malevolent creatures appear in a number of stories in the folklore of the indigenous people of New Zealand.

55.   **Taniwha:** The Maoris will also tell you of Taniwha, beings that inhabit pools or caves by the sea - especially in dangerous areas with strong currents. Some Taniwha are considered protective guardians (known as *kaitiaki*) whereas others are known as dangerous creatures who may even set out to enslave anyone who passes nearby. Interestingly, belief in the existence of these spirits ensured that a major New Zealand highway was re-routed so as not to infringe on the territory of one protective Taniwha.

56.   **Kraken:** First referred to in an Old Icelandic saga called *Orvar-Oddr*, the Kraken is a sea monster of giant proportions. Whereas many have scoffed at tales of a many-legged sea creature of humongous size, the relatively recent discovery of a species we refer to as a colossal squid (which can grow up to fifteen metres long), stories of the Kraken no longer seem as unlikely as they once did! In the very earliest works however, Kraken were in fact described as being more like crabs than squid - perhaps there is still a hitherto unknown enormous sea creature lurking at the bottom of the Greenland Sea as described in the old texts!

57. **Vodyanoy:** This naked old man with a frog's face is prominent in Czech mythology. With his green beard, long hair and body made of black fish scales (which themselves are covered in algae), this creature would drown people and animals when he was angered; to appease him fishermen, millers and even bee-keepers would make sacrifices in his honour.

58. **Incubus:** If you are female and you have ever woken up in the middle of the night unable to move your limbs, it is quite possible that you have been visited by an Incubus. Considered a demon in some cultures, this creature is said to prey on unwilling victims in the middle of the night, his visit almost always accompanied by paralysis of his victim.

59. **Succubus:** If you are male on the other hand, the same symptoms would suggest an encounter with a succubus - also referred to as a *night hag*. As the experience of one's mind being awake whereas the body appears to be asleep is common across all cultures, scientists have looked into the causes of this further. Known as *sleep paralysis*, these 'visits' from incubi or succubi are today explained as being in a particular state half-way between awake and dreaming, in which one often feels pressure on their chest - possibly causing the hallucination of a demon or other creature on top of you... pretty scary stuff!

60. **Orang Pendek:** Another creature akin to *Bigfoot*, Orang Pendek is said to inhabit the mountainous forests on the island of Sumatra. Both locals and visitors to the island have reportedly seen this ape which walks on two feet like a human. Said to be around one metre tall, and covered in grey-brown fur, this legendary creature is in fact said to have a 'high possibility of actual existence' by scientists who have studied the stories of the beast and its local environment.

The Kraken

American & Caribbean

61. **Thunderbird:** The indigenous people of North America tell of an enormous bird that causes the sound of thunder by beating its wings. Sheet lightning is said to be the bird blinking, whereas lightning bolts are made by glowing snakes which the bird carries around with it. The thunderbird is often portrayed as having two horns, and even teeth within its beak.

62. **Chupacabra:** First sighted in Puerto Rico, but with encounters now stretching across the whole of the Americas, the Chupacabra - whose name literally means 'goat sucker' - attacks livestock, drinking their blood. An incredibly modern mythical creature whose first attack occurred in March 1995 (where eight sheep were discovered dead, drained of blood and with puncture wounds in their chests), the Chupacabra is believed to be the size of a small bear, possessing a row of spines across its back and tail.

63. **Skunk Ape:** Essentially the *Bigfoot* of South-eastern USA, the Skunk ape is also referred to as the *Swamp Ape, Stink Ape* or *Myakka Ape*. A foul-smelling hominid, this ape-like creature who walks on two legs has even been captured on camera (although some dispute the photos, saying they have been manipulated).

64.	**Glawackus:** The lumberjacks of early 20th century North America say this creature looked like a cross between a bear, a lion and a panther. Said to have attacked livestock in Connecticut and Massachusetts, the animal has never been caught despite a number of expeditions to find it.

65.	**Nimerigar:** According to the Shoshone people who inhabit the Rocky Mountains in North America, a race of aggressive people called the Nimerigar lived around the Wind River in Wyoming; they were said to fire poisoned arrows at anyone who approached, using tiny well-crafted bows. Although dismissed as legend, in 1932 a mummy was found in a cave nearby which was only fourteen inches tall in height. Scientists put forward a theory that a physical deformity could have manifested itself in the DNA of a community, leading to the common occurrence of this 'miniature' appearance.

66.	**Yacuruna:** If you ever take a trip along the Amazon river, make sure you look out for the Yacuruna. According to the indigenous people of the region, these mythical water people are described as being similar to humans in their form, although their heads are backwards, they are hairier than normal and they have deformed feet. Often accompanied by a river serpent or riding on a crocodile, it is said they roam the rainforest at night, using their ability to turn into an attractive man to entice and capture their victims. The Yacuruna live in upside-down cities in the Amazon river, sleeping on hammocks made from feathers in palaces of crystal with walls covered by pearls and fish scales.

67. **Boo Hag:** In South Carolina and Georgia, people speak in hushed tones of the Boo Hag - a creature much like a vampire, although gaining sustenance from one's breath rather than one's blood. As they have no skin of their own, they will often steal it from their victim, wearing it for as long as it will hold out. You may only be aware that you have been visited by the Boo Hag if you wake up and feel short of breath - or of course if you wake up and you are missing your skin!

68. **Soucouyant:** People of Dominica, Guadeloupe and Trinidad tell of an old woman who lives at the edge of a village but who sheds her skin at night, turning into a fireball to seek victims. Entering their homes through keyholes or cracks in the walls, she sucks people's blood from them whilst they sleep. As well as consuming the blood for nourishment, she also trades for evil witchcraft powers with a demon known as *Bazil* who lives in a silk cotton tree. It is possible to catch one of these creatures by heaping rice at the village crossroads; the Soucouyant will begin to gather it up grain-by-grain at night - a task which takes so long that she can be caught in the act the very next day.

69. **Squonk:** In Pennsylvania at the turn of the 20th century, stories began to circulate of a beast with ill-fitting skin, covered in warts and blemishes which spent most of its time weeping due to its hideous appearance. This creature, known as a Squonk, has an interesting defense mechanism - it is able to dissolve completely into a pool of its own tears when threatened.

70. **Snallygaster:** In the hills around Washington lives the Snallygaster, a Dragon-like beast first spotted by German settlers in the early 18th century. Half lizard, half bird, with a metallic beak full of razor-sharp teeth, this fearsome beast sucked the blood from its victims, and could only be kept at bay by seven pointed stars - which you can still see painted on dwellings in the area today.

The Chupacabra

Classical - Part 2

71. **Mermaid:** In fact, legends of mermaids appear in a great many ancient cultures across Europe, Africa and Asia. With the upper body of a beautiful woman and the tail of a fish, these creatures are purported to have been seen throughout history. In modern times, the pirate Blackbeard reported having seen mermaids in a particular area and therefore demanded his ship be taken a different route, and as recently as 2012, Zimbabwean workers refused to recommence construction on a reservoir, reporting that mermaids had hounded them away from the area.

72. **Siren:** The Sirens lived on islands in the Mediterranean and appeared to be beautiful women who would sing enchanting songs to lure unwary sailors towards them. However, approaching vessels would crash into the rocks around them. Some ancient sources depict the Sirens as having some features of birds, for instance having scaly feet or being covered in feathers. Legend tells of Odysseus and his curiosity as to what the Sirens sounded like; he therefore ordered his men to tie him to his mast, plug their own ears with beeswax, sail past their island and not release him no matter how much he begged. He thus became the only person to have heard their song and lived to tell the tale.

73. **Pegasus:** This winged divine stallion was most often depicted as being pure white in colour; sired by Poseidon and foaled by Medusa, born alongside his brother Chrysaor when his pregnant mother was decapitated by Perseus. In Greek legend, Pegasus was captured by Bellerophon; after a number of adventures however, he fell off the horse's back whilst flying to Mount Olympus. When the horse reached the home of the gods without a rider, Zeus transformed him into a constellation and placed him in the sky.

74. **Gorgon:** These are amongst the oldest creatures described in Greek Mythology, possibly dating back more than three thousand years. Female beings with the ability to turn anyone who laid eyes upon them into stone, the Gorgons (of which later accounts say they were three: *Euryale, Sthenno* and *Medusa*) possessed scales which would deflect any sword, hands made of brass, fangs, beards and of course a hairstyle of living snakes. Sometimes even described as having wings (as if the other terrifying features weren't enough) images of gorgons were often placed on temples and graves to ward away the dark forces of evil.

75. **Sphinx:** Possessing the body of a lion and the head of a human (and sometimes the wings of a bird), the Sphinx would ask a riddle of those who wished to pass; those who could not answer correctly were devoured. Whereas the Greek Sphinx was female and merciless, the Egyptian Sphinx was male and benevolent.

76. **Hydra:** Specifically the *Lernaean Hydra* referred to in the labours of Heracles, this monster had multiple heads, of which should one be cut off, two would grow in its place. With such poisonous breath and blood that even its tracks could kill, the serpent-like creature guarded an entrance to the underworld. It was only defeated when Heracles realised that if he burned the stump of a neck after cutting off a head, none would grow back. Despite a giant crab being sent to get in his way (which the hero stomped to death), Heracles eventually managed to cut off all of the Hydra's heads.

77. **Echidna:** Half winged woman, half snake, the Echidna was known as the 'mother of all monsters'. Authors in ancient times said she bore a number of well-known beasts, including Cerberus, the Chimera, the Gorgons, the Hydra, the Sphinx and more. In one legend, Echidna ate people who passed close to her cave, until one day she was killed by Argus Panoptes, a three-hundred eyed giant.

78. **Giant:** Giants appear in many different folklores. In Greek mythology in particular, they were said to possess great strength - although there is debate as to whether this meant they were large in size. Some representations of the Greek giants - who were said to have battled the Olympian gods - show they have snakes for legs, although this isn't mentioned in classical texts. After being vanquished from the surface of the world, the giants were buried under volcanos, and it is they who cause them to erupt.

79. **Basilisk:** The Basilisk was said to be the king of serpents, a snake that (according to Pliny) was so venomous that it left a deadly trail of poison in its wake and could even kill you with a single glance. It was said that only the smell of a weasel could kill the snake, which surprisingly was supposed to be only around a foot long. In later legends however, the basilisk appears to have grown in size; by medieval times they were said to be able to be killed by gazing at itself in a mirror, or by hearing the crowing of a rooster - leading to some travellers of the age actually carrying roosters around with them! The beast is even referenced in Geoffrey Chaucer's *Canterbury Tales*, although he calls it a *Basilicok*.

80. **Cyclops:** Although the word *Cyclops* in fact means 'round-eyed', this race of giants only had one eye each, according to the Greek author Homer, who tells of how Odysseus blinded the Cyclops Polyphemus with a long stake. Some have speculated that the legend of the Cyclops may have come from ancient people finding the skull of a dwarf elephant; the single hole in its middle (actually for the trunk) would have looked to them like an eye socket in a giant head.

A Mermaid

European - Part 2

81. **Bloody Bones:** Originally hailing from Yorkshire in England, Bloody Bones is said to be a bogeyman that lives in a dark cupboard under the stairs. He preys on young victims, eating their bones which he then uses to make a nest. The earliest reference to Bloody Bones is in the *Oxford English Dictionary* of 1550 in which we are told that the monster is also known to some as *Tommy Rawhead.*

82. **Selkie:** North of mainland Scotland lie two remote island groups called the Orkney and the Shetland isles. Sharing similar folklore, both communities tell of creatures who live as seals in the sea but shed their skin to become human on land. If a man finds a Selkie's skin which she has shed to come on land, she will now be under his power and will become his wife - although as her true home is in the sea she will spend many hours gazing at the ocean. Both male and female Selkies are said to be beautiful, and sometimes seek out those who are dissatisfied with their lives to begin a loving relationship with.

83. **Troll:** In Scandinavian folklore, trolls are said to be ancient and strong but slow and dim-witted. They turn to stone in the sunlight and are dangerous should you come across one at night - trolls will kidnap (and most likely eat) you. In later folk tales it is said that the sound of church bells scares the trolls away from human communities, whereas in earlier legends lightning had the same effect.

84. **Banshee:** This messenger from the underworld takes the form of a fairy woman who wails at an impending death. Important families in Ireland each had their own Banshee, who's mournful cries would signify the imminent passing of one of their members. Whereas some Banshees are said to be terrifyingly ugly, others have been described as beautiful women, and some even as an animal such as a crow, stoat or weasel. Likewise, the Banshee's cry can be anything from a 'low, pleasant singing' to a 'thin, screeching sound somewhere between the wail of a woman and the moan of an owl'.

85. **Valkyrie:** Riding upon winged horses, Valkyries choose slain Norse warriors from the battlefield as their husbands, and bring them to *Valhalla*, the hall ruled over by the god Odin. There, the warriors are served mead and prepare for a huge future battle.

86. **Leprechaun:** Around the height of a small child, with a red beard and clothed in a green suit (although in older days the suit was said to be red), a Leprechaun spends his days making shoes. He is a magical creature who hides his coins in a pot of gold which is stored at the end of a rainbow. When a ladder falls over, a toe is stubbed or another 'unlucky' event occurs, it is actually the fault of the Leprechaun, who loves to play practical jokes on us. If you catch a Leprechaun however, he will grant you three wishes in exchange for his release - although choose wisely, as things don't always turn out the way you plan...

87.	**Ratatoskr:** Ratatoskr is a squirrel from Norse mythology who carries messages up and down the world tree *Yggdrasil* between *Hraesvelgr* (the eagle perched at the top) and *Niohoggr* (the wyrm who lives underneath its roots).

88.	**Grindylow:** Should a child get too close to a lake, a Grindylow with its long, sinewy arms will reach out and pull them in. Hailing from Yorkshire and Lancashire, the word Grindylow is thought to be associated with that of *Grendel*, a giant referenced in the epic poem *Beowulf* who is feared by all but the hero himself.

89.	**Glas Gaibhnenn:** This mythical beast comes from Irish folklore. A white cow covered in green spots, she is said to yield profuse quantities of milk for its owner.

90.	**Kelpie:** Usually appearing as a horse (but in fact able to take on the form of a man or woman), this creature is a common water spirit inhabiting lochs and pools of water in Scotland. Similar to a *Ceffyl Dŵr*, they are said to be mischievous but rarely dangerous to humans (although, like its Welsh counterpart, you shouldn't approach one in case it tramples you to death, devours your carcass and throws your entrails to the water's edge). One question people often ask is how you can tell a Kelpie from a normal horse; the best way to do this is to look at the hooves - a Kelpie's are backwards!

Valkyries

The Most Amazing Creatures

91. **Cipactli:** The Aztecs spoke of a primeval sea monster who was always hungry. Part fish, part crocodile and part toad, every joint on his body was said to have a mouth!

92. **Jenny Greenteeth:** With her sharp green incisors, Jenny Greenteeth lies beneath the surface of lonely water, ready to pull in any inquisitive child who comes too close to the edge. Sometimes, algae can grow over the surface of a pond making it look like a particularly well-manicured lawn; in legend this is said to be the hair of Jenny Greenteeth, who will quickly roll over and grab you should you decide to take a closer look!

93. **Moon Rabbit:** In both East Asian and Aztec mythology, it was said that a rabbit lived on the moon - this was based on the satellite's markings, which some thought looked like a rabbit grinding and pounding using a pestle and mortar. The Chinese say it is concocting the elixir of life, whereas the Japanese and Koreans believe it is making tasty rice cakes. One Chinese legend tells of how a girl named Chang-o was banished to the moon for stealing the pill or immortality from her husband; she managed to take her pet rabbit with her and they have been living there ever since. Fantastically, the astronauts of Apollo 11 were told to look out for the girl before the 1969 moon landing!

94. **Jimmy Squarefoot:** Usually peaceful, this creature with a pig's head wanders around the Isle of Man reared up on his two hind legs. His enormous feet are square in appearance and was once the steed of the *Foawr*, a local race of giants.

95. **Will-o'-the-Wisp:** Also known to some as *Jack-o'-Lantern,* these ghost lights float a few feet above the surface of the marshes and resemble a flickering gas lamp. Should a traveller stray from the safe path to take a closer look at one of these intriguing lights, the flame recedes and the 'victim' will more than likely be stuck in the boggy ground until he perishes. Some believe that there is a scientific explanation for the will-o'-the-wisps; that naturally occurring swamp gas ignites and slowly burns, causing the effect. Others however say there is a more supernatural explanation, and that the lights are the souls of the dead.

96. **Näkki:** Just like Jenny Greenteeth, a Näkki lives under the surface of the water, ready to pull young children to their deaths should they lean a little too far over bridges or railings that cross rivers in Finland. Said to appear as a beautiful woman from the front, but a hideous hairy fish-man from the rear, this shape-shifter can even transform into a fish, horse or dog at will. If you want to see a Näkki without dying, perhaps your best chance is to visit the country on Midsummers night, when they are said to rise up from the water to dance and join the local celebrations.

97. **Mongolian Death Worm:** Said to inhabit the Gobi desert, this red worm grows up to five feet long and can spew an acid that can kill a human and will even corrode metal. Not only does it possess this unusual ability, but it can also electrocute victims at will from a distance. Amazingly, this is another mythical beast referenced in this book for which many expeditions have set out attempting to locate it... *It is thought that this creature could well exist!*

98. **Gashadokuro:** Surely one of the most frightening beasts in this book, Gashadokuro are giant skeletons of Japanese legend, fifteen times the height of a normal man. As soon as it spots a human, this terrifying entity will grab them and bite their head off, enjoying and drinking the spray of blood that this act creates. If this wasn't scary enough, the Gashadokuro can also make themselves invisible (and indestructible) and target people when they are alone - however, a sure sign of one approaching is that you will hear an extremely loud ringing of bells in your ears.

99. **Cockatrice:** Mentioned in English myths dating back centuries, the magical cockatrice looked like a two-legged Dragon with the head of a rooster. It was supposedly born from an egg that had been laid by a chicken but incubated by a toad, and had the ability to turn people to stone with its gaze, just like a *Basilisk*. If one found an egg suspected of containing a cockatrice, the best way to prevent it from hatching was to throw it all the way over your house, ensuring it didn't hit anything during its high trajectory.

100. **Manticore:** Similar to the *Sphinx*, the Manticore had the body of a lion and the head of a human - although this beast of Persian mythology was also said to have three rows of shark's teeth, the wings of a bat, the tail of a scorpion and a voice that sounded like a trumpet. It could kill its victims by shooting poisonous spines at them, then devouring its prey whole not leaving a single bone behind. The Manticore should not be confused with the *Mantiger* (or *Mantyger*) popular in medieval bestiaries, which had the body of a tiger, the head of a man and the feet of a monkey.

A Manticore

And Finally...

101. **Slenderman:** Some people will tell you that Slenderman is an invention of the internet - and as mythical creatures go, that would be quite interesting by itself. However, legends of a tall, thin skeletal figure have persisted for years across many cultures, even if they don't have the abilities that current Slenderman mythos attributes - being able to cause *Slender Sickness* for instance. Said to sleep on a bed of dirt taken from a fresh grave, or to inhabit a fetid well near to his intended victims, Slenderman is a truly terrifying mythical beast worthy of inclusion on any list of creatures of legend.

CPSIA information can be obtained at www.ICGtesting.com
Printed in the USA
LVOW07s0851021015

456655LV00001B/14/P